Letter Stickers

Put these stickers at the top of the pages where they belong.

 m
 t

 r
 n
 d
 p

 s
 k
 b
 l

 f
 c
 c
 j

 h
 g
 g
 y

 v
 w
 z
 q

More stickers at back of book!

Beginning m

 and  begin with the sound for the letter **m**.

 Name each picture.
Write **m** to finish each word. Say the word.

an   ilk   ice

___ask   ___oon   ___op

Put **m** stickers next to the pictures that start with **m**.

Skill: Recognizing initial consonant **m**.

Beginning t

 and  begin with the sound for the letter **t**.

✏️ Name the pictures in each row.
Circle the pictures that start with **t**.

t	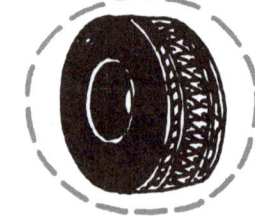			
t				
t				

✏️ Trace each word. Say the word.

  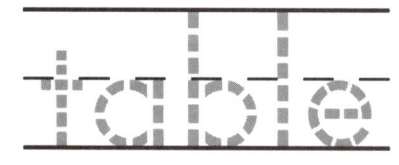 

Skill: Recognizing initial consonant **t**.

Beginning r

 and begin with the sound for the letter **r**.

 Name each picture.
Color the pictures of words that start with **r**.

Read the rhyming words.
Find the stickers that show the words that begin with **r**.

bed	**red**	**bug**	**rug**

king	**ring**	**nose**	**rose**

Skill: Recognizing initial consonant **r**.

Beginning n

 and  begin with the sound for the letter **n**.

✏️ Find and color 7 things that begin with **n**.

 Write 2 words that start with **n**.

_____   _____

4 Skill: Recognizing initial consonant **n**.

Beginning d

 and begin with the sound for the letter **d**.

 Name each picture. Draw lines from the  to the pictures that start with **d**.

 Trace the words.

 Find the stickers.

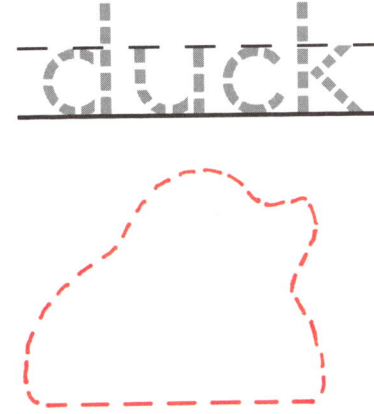

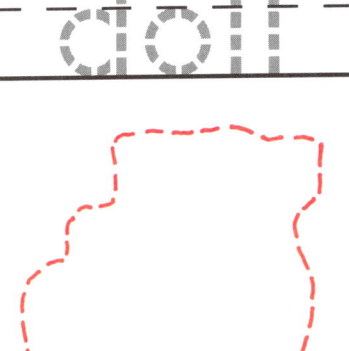

Skill: Recognizing initial consonant **d**.

Beginning p

🦜 and ✏️ begin with the sound for the letter **p**.

✏️ Write **p** to finish each word.

✏️ Find the pictures that show the words. Color them. Then say the words.

p ig

_ ie

_ iano

_ illow

_ ail

6   Skill: Recognizing initial consonant **p**.

Beginning s

 and 🧼 begin with the sound for the letter **s**.

✎ Name each picture.
Write **s** to finish each word. Say the word.

s aw   __un    __ail

__ock    __ix 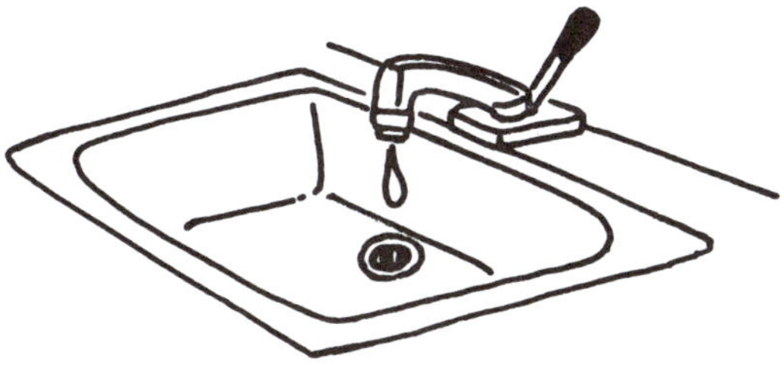   __ink

 Put **s** stickers next to the pictures that start with **s**.

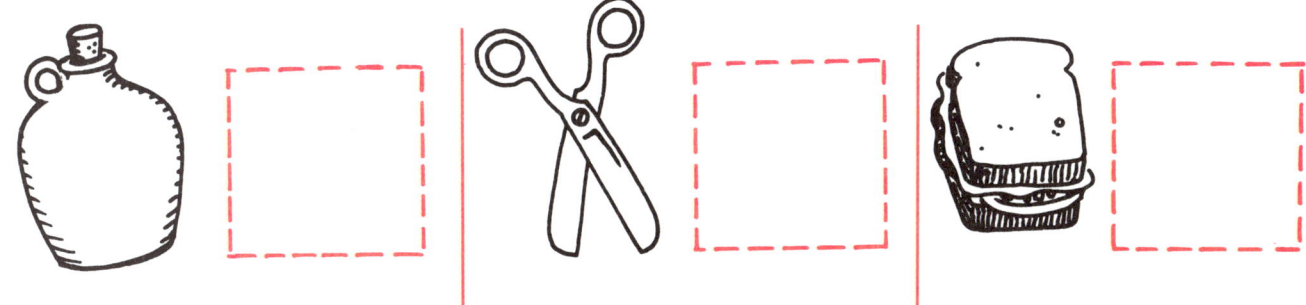

Skill: Recognizing initial consonant **s**.

Beginning k

 and begin with the sound for the letter **k**.

 Name each picture.
Write **k** to finish each word. Say the word.

Key   _ite   _ing

 Find the pictures of the words you just wrote. Color them.

 Find and color 3 more words that start with **k**.

Skill: Recognizing initial consonant **k**.

Beginning b

 and  begin with the sound for the letter **b**.

Name the pictures in each row.
Circle the pictures that start with **b**.

Trace each word. Say the word.

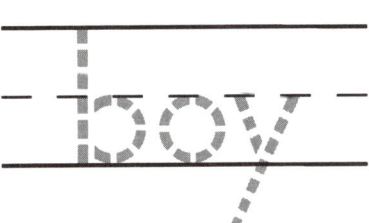     

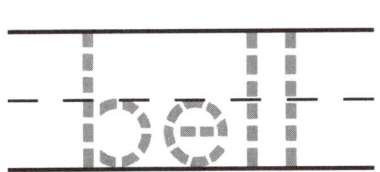    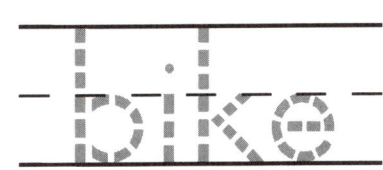 

 Answer the riddle with a sticker.

What has a head and a foot but no body?

Skill: Recognizing initial consonant **b**.

Beginning l

 and  begin with the sound for the letter **l**.

✏️ Write **l** to finish each word.

🖍️ Find the pictures that show the words. Color them. Then say the words.

l og

_ eaf

_ amb

_ ock

_ adder

Skill: Recognizing initial consonant l.

Beginning f

 and  begin with the sound for the letter **f**.

 Name each picture.
Write **f** to finish each word. Say the word.

fire

___an

___ish

___ive

 Find the pictures of the words you just wrote. Color them.

 Find and color 3 more words that start with **f**.

Skill: Recognizing initial consonant **f**.

Beginning c

 and   begin with the sound for the letter **c**.

✏️ Write **c** to make a word that rhymes with the first one.

🧽 Find the stickers.

rake   c ake

boat   _ oat

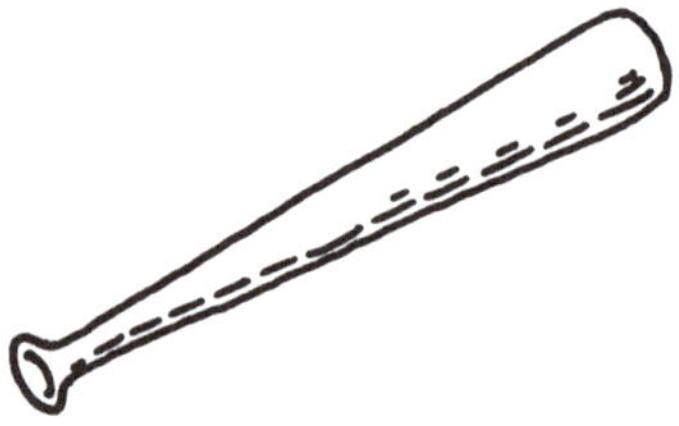

bat   _ at

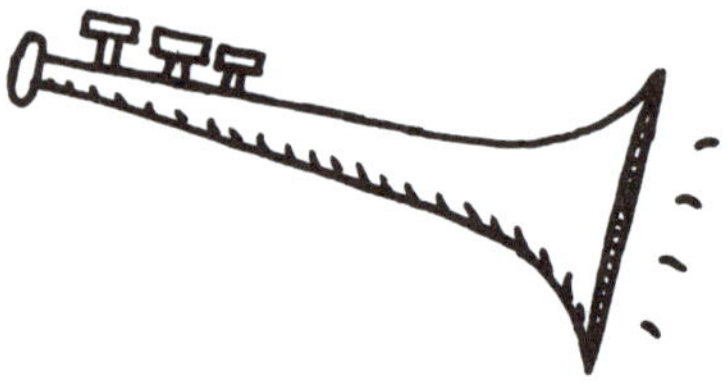

horn   _ orn

12   Skill: Recognizing initial consonant **c**.

Beginning c

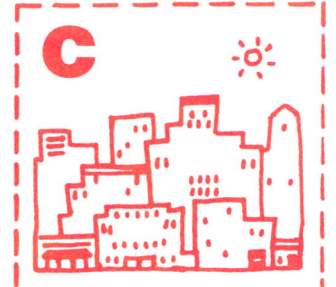

Sometimes the letter **c** has the **s** sound. It stands for the sound at the beginning of 🏙️.

**Name each picture.
Write c under the ones that start like 🏙️.**

Skill: Recognizing initial consonant c (soft c).

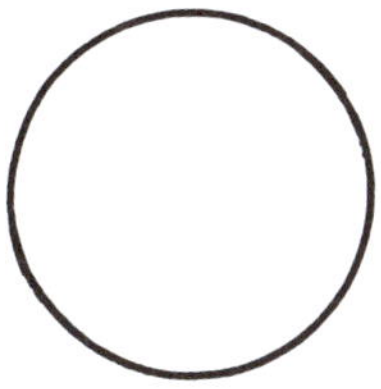

Beginning j

 and  begin with the sound for the letter **j**.

 Name each picture.
Color the pictures of words that start with **j**.

 Write **j** to make a word that rhymes with the first one.

 Find the stickers.

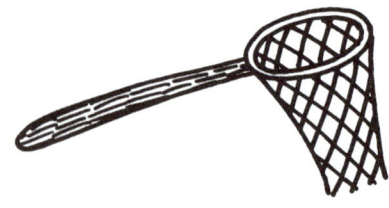 net   _ _et

 ham   _ _am

Skill: Recognizing initial consonant **j**.

I'm Tommy Tiger, and T is my song.
I make up tunes about T all day long!
I beat on tom-toms, and tap my feet,
and toot on a tuba, and sing, "T is neat!"

I'm Betty Bear, and B is my letter!
Bs make everything taste much better.
I love berries that are big and blue,
and I love honey from beehives, too!

I'm Ricky Rabbit—I run after Rs!
I chase roller coasters and red race cars.
I run like a rocket—I'm not at all slow,
and when I see an R, it means "ready, set, go!"

I'm Danny Dog, I think Ds are dandy!
Ds are delicious—they taste like candy.
Devil's food cake has a D, and it's sweet,
just like the donuts I have here to eat!

I'm Penny Pig, and I'm poking for Ps!
This pantry has plenty of pastries for me.
I can see pumpkin and pecan pies,
and the popcorn up there is a feast for
  my eyes.

I'm Gary Goat—I'm a G kind of guy!
I gather Gs and I keep them nearby.
I play my guitar by the garden gate,
and gobble up grapes from a golden plate.

I'm Linda Lamb, and as you can tell,
I think the letter L is swell!
I lick lollipops and wear a lace cap,
and listen to lullabies on my mom's lap.

Beginning h

 and 🍔 begin with the sound for the letter **h**.

✏️ Name the pictures in each row.
Circle the pictures that start with **h**.

✏️ Trace each word. Say the word.

Skill: Recognizing initial consonant **h**.

Beginning g

 and 🎁 begin with the sound for the letter **g**.

✏️ Name each picture. Draw lines from the 👻 to the pictures that start with **g**.

✏️ Look at each picture. Write a word that starts with **g** to finish each rhyme.

a _____ in a coat

a loose _____

20   Skill: Recognizing initial consonant g.

Beginning g

Sometimes the letter **g** has the **j** sound. It stands for the sound at the beginning of .

 Name each picture.
Write **g** under the ones that start like .

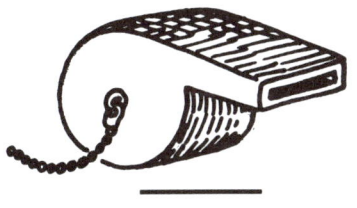

Skill: Recognizing initial consonant **g** (soft **g**).

Beginning y

 and  begin with the sound for the letter y.

Trace each word. Say the word.

 Answer the riddle with a sticker.

What goes up and down but never gives you a ride?

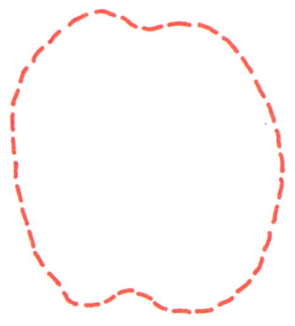

22 Skill: Recognizing initial consonant **y**.

Beginning v

and  begin with the sound for the letter **v**.

Find and color 7 things that begin with **v**.

 Write 2 words that start with **v**.

_____   _____

Skill: Recognizing initial consonant **v**.   23

Beginning w

 and  begin with the sound for the letter **w**.

 Name the pictures in each row.
Circle the pictures that start with **w**.

W
W

 Look at each picture.
Write a word that starts with **w** to finish each rhyme.

a pig in a _____

a dragon in a _____

Skill: Recognizing initial consonant **w**.

Beginning z

 begins with the sound for the letter **z**.

 Name each picture.
Color the pictures that start with **z**.

 Trace the words.

 Find the stickers.

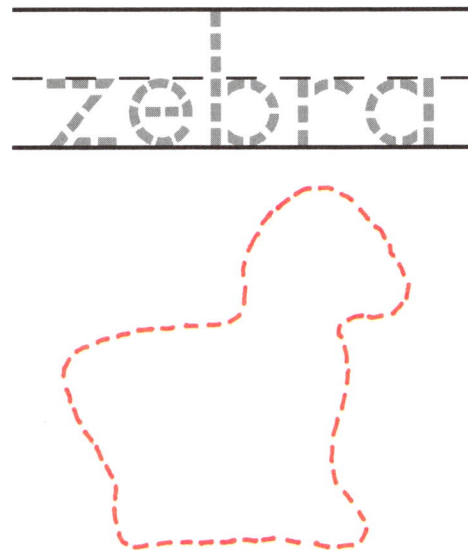

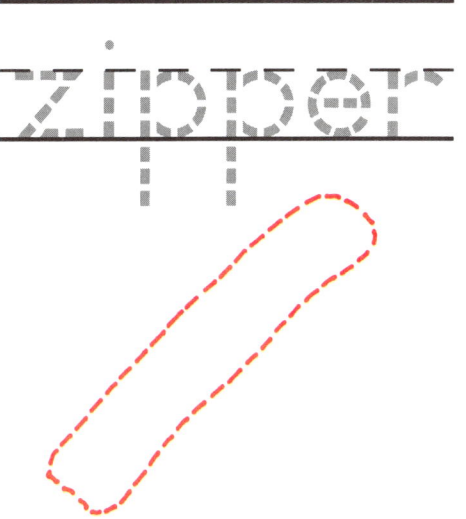

Skill: Recognizing initial consonant z.

Beginning q

 and ? begin with the sound for the letter **q**.

 Name each picture.
Draw lines from the ? to the pictures that start with **q**.

 Trace each word. Say the word.

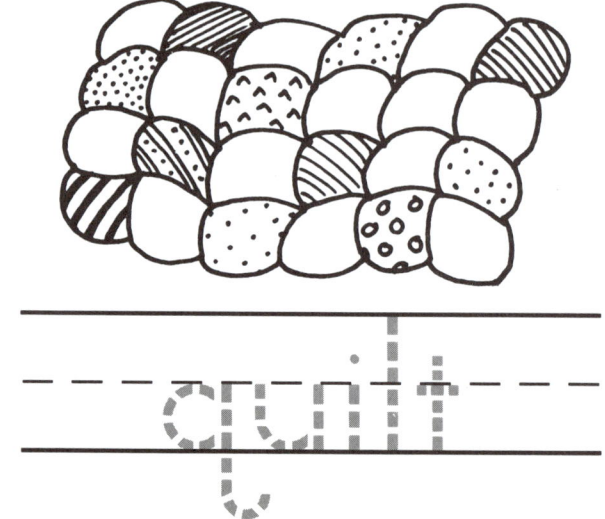

Skill: Recognizing initial consonant **q**.

Endings: d, g

The words in each box have the same ending sound.

 be**d**    sa**d**    fla**g**    pi**g**

 Name the first picture in the row.
Color the pictures that end with the same sound.

 Name each picture.
Write **d** or **g** to finish each word. Say the word.

      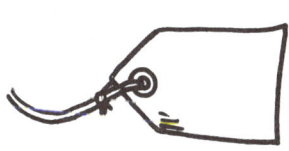

do __   bir __   ta __

      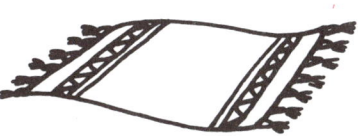

bu __   hea __   ru __

Skill: Recognizing final consonants **d** and **g**.   27

Endings: n, t

The words in each box have the same ending sound.

 Name each picture.
Write **n** or **t** to finish each word. Say the word.

te __   su __   po __

ha __   pe __   je __

 Color the pictures of words that end with the letter in each box.

Endings: p, x

The words in each box have the same ending sound.

 ma<u>p</u>  soa<u>p</u>    o<u>x</u>    si<u>x</u>

 Name the first picture in the row.
Color the pictures that end with the same sound.

 Name each picture.
Write **p** or **x** to finish each word. Say the word.

to ___   mi ___   ca ___

si ___   bo ___   cu ___

Skill: Recognizing final consonants **p** and **x**.

Endings: ll, ss

The words in each box have the same ending sound.

 bell  doll    dre**ss**  gra**ss**

 Name each picture.
Write **ll** or **ss** to finish each word. Say the word.

gla____   ba____   gra____

hi____   ki____   do____

 Read the sentences. Find the stickers.

Pass the ball.   **The glass is full.**

Practice Test

 Name each picture.
Fill in the circle next to the letter for the beginning sound.

○ m
● t
○ r

○ n
○ p
○ d

○ r
○ f
○ l

○ n
○ k
○ p

○ c
○ s
○ w

○ x
○ q
○ z

○ g
○ v
○ w

○ s
○ k
○ b

○ t
○ m
○ j

○ j
○ h
○ y

○ p
○ d
○ f

○ s
○ y
○ l

Skill: Testing beginning consonant sounds.

Practice Test

 Name each picture.
Fill in the circle next to the letter(s) for the ending sound.

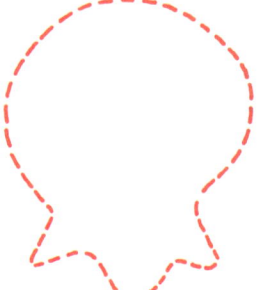

Picture	Choices
	● d ○ g ○ t
	○ t ○ n ○ p
	○ g ○ x ○ t
	○ ss ○ x ○ p
	○ g ○ d ○ t
	○ t ○ d ○ p
	○ ss ○ ll ○ d
	○ p ○ x ○ t
	○ ss ○ t ○ ll
	○ t ○ d ○ g
	○ ll ○ d ○ ss
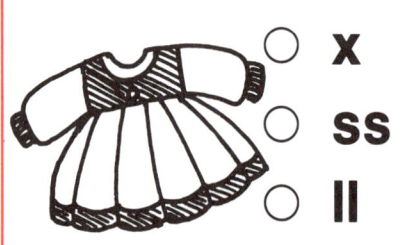	○ x ○ ss ○ ll

32   Skill: Testing final consonant sounds.

page 5

page 9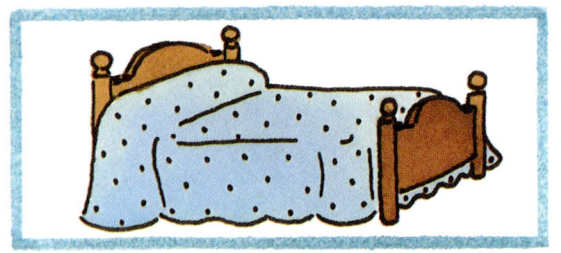

page 30

page 14

page 1

page 3

page 12

page 7

Reward Stickers!

page 25

page 32

page 31

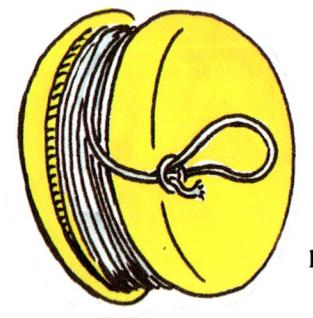
page 22